THIS WALKER BOOK BELONGS TO:

_____

_____

_____

_____

For Jenny Hawkesworth *M.C.*
For Elizabeth *C.G.*

First published 1980 by Walker Books Ltd
87 Vauxhall Walk, London SE11 5HJ

This edition published 1989

Text © 1980 Mirabel Cecil
Illustrations © 1980 Christina Gascoigne

Printed in Italy by Lito di Roberto Terrazzi

British Library Cataloguing in Publication Data
Cecil, Mirabel
Ruby the donkey.
I. Title II. Gascoigne, Christina
823'.9'1J   PZ10.3
ISBN 0-7445-1362-6

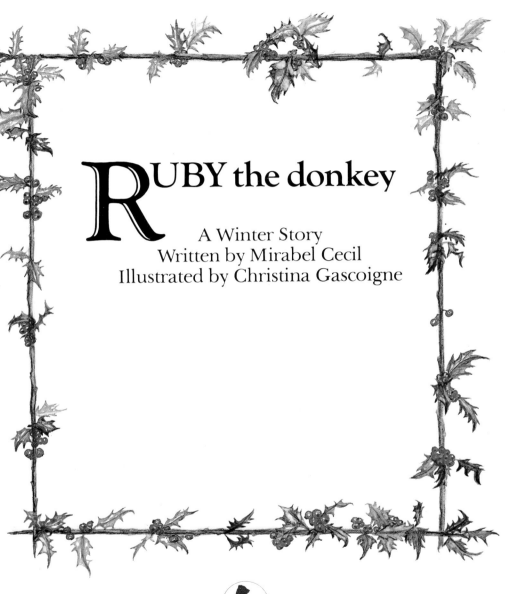

# RUBY the donkey

A Winter Story
Written by Mirabel Cecil
Illustrated by Christina Gascoigne

WALKER BOOKS
LONDON

Ruby and Scarlett were two donkeys who spent their summers giving rides to children on the beach.

They had been doing this for many years, especially Ruby, who was the older of the two donkeys.

But one summer, Ruby was not chosen for rides nearly as often as Scarlett. Ruby was not as strong as she had been, and could only plod slowly along the sands. So Scarlett carried the children, while Ruby waited for her to come back.

Much of the time, Ruby stood alone.

Both the donkeys looked forward to the end of summer. They knew they would spend a peaceful autumn in a field.

Old Ruby was particularly pleased at the good rest.

Sometimes the children who lived nearby came to see Ruby and Scarlett. They brought the donkeys crusts and carrots to eat.

Ruby moved more and more slowly.

Winter came. The little creatures
who lived nearby grew warm coats
or got ready to sleep through the
cold months.

Ruby was too old to grow a warm coat.

"Why not run round as I do?" said Scarlett. But Ruby could not.

Tears trickled down Ruby's soft, grey
nose. They turned to icicles before
they reached the ground.

Ruby bowed her shaggy, old head in the bitter wind. She thought of the hot summers she had spent on the beach, and wondered whether she would ever enjoy the sunshine again.

"I never thought I would end my days in this cold misery," she complained to Scarlett.

The little animals were usually fast asleep now, but they could not rest while their old friend Ruby was so unhappy. They decided that since she could not make a warm winter coat for herself, they would make one for her!

Mice collected
pine cones, birds got pine
needles and hares made piles of wool.

The mole woke up. The dormice, shrew
and birds put everything
into heaps.

Rabbits hopped quickly to the hares with wool from the sheep while hedgehogs and rats gathered leaves.

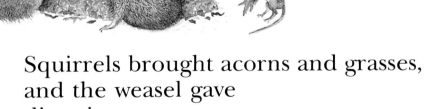

Squirrels brought acorns and grasses, and the weasel gave directions.

Soon it was time to make the coat.
Hedgehogs, mice, rats and squirrels
wove the grasses on to a branch.

The birds used their beaks to add
the feathers, wool and leaves.
At last the coat was finished!

The weasel blew his whistle to wake the owl, who was big enough and strong enough to lift up the coat.

The owl picked up the coat with the help of the other birds.

Silently, they flew off.

Ruby lay on the frosty ground,
trying to keep warm. She did not
hear the swish of the birds' wings,
or see the weasel directing the owl.

Ruby did not even notice all the animals gathered round her.

When the birds dropped the coat
on to her, Ruby first thought it was
a present that had fallen out of the
snowy sky.

It was a wonderful coat, a magic coat!
  "Now I'll never be cold again,"
Ruby said, as she thanked all the
animals.

The next day the children came
down to the field with carrots and
crusts for the donkeys. They were
going to choose one donkey to be in
a Nativity play they were giving that
night.

Would it be Scarlett? Or Ruby?

Last year Scarlett had been chosen,
and so now she came forward
eagerly to the gate. But one of the
boys noticed Ruby's coat at once.

"Look!" he shouted to the others.
"Look at Ruby's magic coat! We
must have her in the Nativity play!"

So the children led Ruby out of the
field towards the school where
everyone was busy getting ready for
the play.

Scarlett and the other animals
watched as Ruby left. They were
very proud of the coat they had
made her.

That night, as snow fell softly, all the animals went up to the school. They gathered round the lighted window to watch the play. Even the mole managed to stay awake. And the weasel made sure that everyone was quiet.

They saw all the children dressed in their costumes. But Ruby did not have to dress up. She was perfect as she was, in her magic coat, with the peacock feathers that glowed like jewels.

Best of all, Ruby would never be
cold again. She had her coat of wool
and feathers, and grasses and leaves.

# MORE WALKER PAPERBACKS

## BABIES' FIRST BOOKS
### Jan Ormerod
**Little ones**
JUST LIKE ME
SILLY GOOSE    OUR OLLIE

## PICTURE BOOKS
**For the very young**

### Helen Oxenbury
**Pippo**
No.1 TOM & PIPPO READ A STORY
No.2 TOM & PIPPO MAKE A MESS
No.3 TOM  & PIPPO GO FOR A WALK
No.4 TOM & PIPPO AND THE
    WASHING MACHINE
No.5 TOM & PIPPO GO SHOPPING
No.6 TOM & PIPPO'S DAY
No.7 TOM & PIPPO IN THE GARDEN
No.8 TOM & PIPPO SEE THE MOON

### Nicola Bayley
BEDTIME RHYMES
NONSENSE RHYMES

## LEARNING FOR FUN
**The Pre-School Years**

### Shirley Hughes
**Nursery Collection**
NOISY
COLOURS
BATHWATER'S HOT
ALL SHAPES AND SIZES
TWO SHOES, NEW SHOES
WHEN WE WENT TO THE PARK

### John Burningham
**Concept Books**
COLOURS   ALPHABET
OPPOSITES   NUMBERS

### Philippe Dupasquier
**Busy Places**
THE GARAGE    THE AIRPORT
THE BUILDING SITE
THE FACTORY    THE HARBOUR
THE RAILWAY STATION